PAWA

The Unlawful Love

A Tale Of Hidden Romance

First edition

This book was professionally typeset on Reedsy.
Find out more at reedsy.com

Contents

FREE BOOK

Interested in more forbidden love stories, download 10 FREE Short Romance short stories here and sign up for my mailing list to find out when the next book comes out.

https://bit.ly/PawaFreeRomanceBook

OR

Scan the barcode below

One

A College Sweetheart

The looming sunlight invaded the heavy mountains and reached the town's lowermost corners. This was an ordinary spring for the people living in Alpine, Switzerland. The flashy green grass and strong hailing winds were welcoming spring. The cluttering of people and chirping of birds in the field of Alpine was already witnessing the smoothness that comes with Spring. Here, Ayla and Levin were waiting to welcome their first child. Laying in the hospital bed Ayla was looking at the heavy mirrors that were welcoming sunlight. It was a perfect day as Ayla thought while looking at the high clouds wavering in the blue sky.

As Ayla lay in the hospital bed, she couldn't help but feel grateful for her husband Levin, who sat beside her, holding her hand. Despite the excitement of welcoming their first child, Ayla couldn't shake the nervousness she felt about becoming a parent. Sensing her anxiety, Levin leaned in and placed a gentle kiss on her forehead.

"You're going to be an amazing mother," he whispered, his warm breath sending shivers down her spine.

Ayla smiled, feeling a wave of love wash over her. She couldn't imagine going through this experience with anyone else by her side. Levin leaned in closer to Ayla, his eyes filled with love and adoration. He gently brushed a strand of hair away from her face, taking in every detail of her beauty. He had never felt so deeply in love with anyone before, and he couldn't believe how lucky he was to have Ayla as his wife.

"You are the most beautiful thing I have ever seen," he whispered, his voice barely above a breath.

Ayla's heart skipped a beat as she gazed into Levin's deep, soulful eyes. She had always known that he was the one for her, but at this moment, she felt an even deeper connection with him. She felt like they were the only two people in the world, and nothing else mattered.

Levin gently cupped Ayla's face in his hands and brought his lips to hers. Their kiss was slow and tender, filled with all the love they had for each other. As they broke apart, Ayla could feel tears prickling at the corners of her eyes.

"I love you so much, Levin," she whispered, her voice trembling with emotion.

Levin smiled, his heart swelling with happiness. He knew that Ayla was the missing piece in his life, and he never wanted to let her go. He took her hand in his and squeezed it gently, silently promising to always be there for her no matter what.

As they sat there together, basking in the glow of their love, they knew that they had something truly special. They had a love that would stand the test of time, a love that was deep, pure, and unbreakable.

At that very moment, Ayla threw a sharp scream while holding her baby bump. She felt a sharp pain down there and immediately asked for help. There was pain and happiness on her face at the same time. Seeing his beloved getting into labor, Levin rushed to get medical help to assist his dearest wife. As he went back Ayla managed to get herself on the bed. The doctor examined her real quick and Levin stood by comforting his warrior wife.

"You are eight centimeters dilated, Miss Ayla, this is the time you need to push. The doctor said while holding down a pair of surgical thongs in his hands

"You are my warrior Ayla! My love, you can do it." Levin looked at Ayla with all of his love and whispered straight in her ears while gently sealing a kiss on her forehead.

Ayla held his hand with her attire and began to push the baby out of her womb. It almost took an hour for her to give birth. Finally, the words of the doctor made her relieved as he uttered that the baby is here! Ayla was drenched in blood, sweat and pain but it was the day she entered motherhood. Levin cut down the umbilical cord of the baby while saying,

"Honey! It's a girl…" with tears of happiness and joy in their eyes.

Ayla held her little princess in her hands and immediately named her Lila. Lila was just the perfect little creature that Ayla and Levin have longed for. They took Lila to their home down the lane and every single pain was replaced by the cheerful Lila. She brought happiness and beauty to her parents' lives. Years passed by and Lila was being raised by a strong businesswoman who used to work 8 to 12 hours a day at the cheese farm.

Ayla was a certified cheese professional who was working vigorously on testing and manufacturing some new products. Ayla was a wise and sensitive mother who raised Lila with all the best parenting traits. On the other hand, Levin was a full-time surgeon who worked for the city hospital. He was there for her beloved daughter teaching her some surgical techniques. And here comes Lila. She was the perfect blend of two of them. She inherited bright red hair, a sharp nose, a bright skin tone from her mother, and bright blue eyes with an incredible smile from her father. Nonetheless, Lila was raised with love and passion.

She grew up idolizing her parent's love story. The way they stand for each other and how her father treats her mother at home. For Lila, the only form of love that existed is just like her parent's love for each other. As time flew, Lila grew up and she was 18 years old, who successfully secured admission to the College. She was all excited about getting into college as it was her time to find a perfect soul mate. Lila grew up under the calm shadow of her parent's love story that always restrained her from getting a boyfriend.

Despite the fact that Lila won't share that much time with her parents, Ayla and Levin always manage to take care of her. The two of them were obsessed with their careers, but at the same time, they were struggling in giving some time to their daughter. Unlike the other children in the neighborhood, Lila was there sitting in her living room watching and reading the love letters that were once written by her parents to express their passion towards each other. This morning, Lila received a notification from Central University. She opened up the email:

"Dear Lila,

On behalf of Central University, I am pleased to inform you that your application for admission has been accepted. Congratulations! We are confident that you will excel in your academic pursuits and contribute positively to our university community. We were impressed by your academic achievements, extracurricular activities, and personal statement.

Your dedication and hard work have clearly paid off, and we believe that you will thrive in our challenging academic environment. We look forward to welcoming you to our campus and supporting you throughout your academic journey. Please let us know if you have any questions or concerns. We are here to help.

Sincerely,"

Lila screamed with joy and was waiting for her parents to spill the news. She waited there till night and spent her time baking her mother's favorite pie. Ayla and Levin stepped into the house. The two of them hugged each other in order to revive their long lasting love. At that very moment, there was the aroma of freshly baked pie with appetizing cherry topping.

"I think we are having a perfect pie for tonight!" Levin said while hugging his dear wife.

Ayla smiled and the two of them walked down the kitchen where Lila was singing and doing some final touches.

"Lila! Honey….." Ayla called her as she was totally merged in her cooking.

"Oh, hey mom! Hey dad!!! Look, I cooked so much mud pie for you…." Laila said with a smile on her face while she was still wearing an apron with a piping bag filled with fresh cream.

"Well! Our daughter must have something to tell us. Right!" Levin said while kissing Lila's forehead.

"Umm! Yesss, I want you to sit by and hear me out…" Lila said while giving some final touches.

The two of them comforted themselves at the dinner table. Lila went to the living room and bought a laptop with her. She turned the screen towards her parents. It was the admission confirmation email from the university.

Levin and Ayla glanced at the context and stood there in silence. There was no immediate reaction as Lila was expecting that they would be happy.

"What happened?" Lila asked with curiosity on her face.

"You can't go there, honey…." Ayla said in return.

"But why? Why are you saying this to me?" Lila groaned.

"Honey! Your mother is right.." Levin added

"Mom and Dad, you know that it's my dream college and I always want to get in there…." Lila said with half teary eyes. Without listening to a word Lila left and locked herself in her room. The next morning she received a letter with enchanted words that pushed her happiness to the seventh sky.

Two

Mr. Hunky

Sun was up high, the glamorous rays welcoming another day. The chirping sound of birds knocking against the window. And all of a sudden here comes a ringing……

It was Lila's alarm clock slackening the bells as it was 7 am in the morning. Laila woke up on the first bell. Lowering her hand out of sheets she snuggled and turned off the alarm. It was another shiny sunny morning in March, two days before Lila's birthday. Last night has been quite hectic for her as her parent's disapproval had almost taken her life away. Lila was still alive but buried under the heavy burden of her versatile dreadful dreams. There was a knock at her room's door.

Lila knew who was there but she stood in silence. After three knocks a voice raised,

"Lila! My only one. Come downstairs, your mom and I are waiting for you." Levin said with a humble tone.

Levin stood there and waited for Lila's reply. But she didn't bother answering. It was quite clear that Lila was really mad at them. Levin stood there and knocked on the door once again.

"The door is open, dad!" Lila said while she snuggled back in her sheets.

Levin walked in and saw that her room was all messed up. Lila has never been a messy girl but only when she goes insane about something. The usually pristine space was in complete disarray. Clothes were strewn about the room, papers were scattered across the floor, and the bed was unmade with the sheets twisted and crumpled. Levin couldn't help but feel a twinge of concern as he saw his daughter's state of mind reflected in the mess. He had always been proud of Lila's responsible and organized nature, and this sudden change was troubling. As he surveyed the room, he noticed a piece of paper on the ground. He picked it up and saw that it was an acceptance letter from University that was being torn due to extreme distress. Levin's heart sank as he realized the reason for Lila's distress. He knew that she had been dreaming of attending that university for years, but he and his wife had been hesitant to let her go.

Feeling guilty and conflicted, Levin decided that he needed to have a conversation with Lila and figure out a way to support her dreams while also ensuring her safety and well-being. But for now, he simply stood in the messy room, taking in the sight and trying to understand his daughter's emotions. Seeing Lila in her bed hiding her face, was evident that she was not in the mood for anything. Levin being an attentive dad stood by her bed and began to cuddle her hair saying

"My love! The day you were born me and your mom were high in the sky. You are a miracle child, the only one we own. Your mother won't conceive a child as per some health, but when it was you we threw every single thing and turned ourselves in raising you my daughter. Just like you, your mom is just as miserable as you are." Levin said with all his love.

The kind words of her father were compatible enough to let her shed the anger Lila holds. She slipped out of the bed and immediately hugged her father.

"I am sorry for throwing a tantrum like a 5 year old. But father, I really want to get in there. I know, I applied there without your consent and sending me away was never on the list. But I am grown and I promise I will be here every weekend……" Lila sounds pretty convincing. Levin looked at his daughter and smiled.

"Your mom and I are downstairs honey." Levin said as he gently kissed his daughter's forehead.

Lila was clear with her words and now all she expected was a permission from her parents to attend the college. Despite her clear words, there was no immediate reaction by Levin, which means that she will be needing another seat with her parents in order to bring them on one page . Gathering her courage Lila, dressed herself nicely, went for some refreshment, comb her hair and was all gathered up to convince her parents. With a slow pace she stumbled down the stairs without making a noise to look at what her parents were doing in the living room. As she sneaked out her mother was washing the dishes and Levin was helping her in cleaning.

"Good morning sweetheart!" Ayla said while she wiped her hands off. Lila stood there and greeted her parents.

"Without wasting any time, honey I have something that I would like you to see. Come here!" Ayla said while pointing towards the table complementing the living area interior. Ayla sat with her daughter Lila and Levin made himself comfortable next to them.

"These are some hostels and apartments your mother and I have enlisted." Lila looked at them. Levin said and handed her the pamphlets. Lila was shocked by what's happening here. She glanced upon the coupons that brought a huge smile on her face.

"Mom, is this for real!" Lila said while hugging her mother with all her love. Ayla whispered back in her daughter's ears saying tomorrow will be your first day honey. Pack your stuff.

Lila jumped out of the couch and handed the coupons to her father and asked him to decide her residence. It was Sunday morning and Ayla packed herself with all the essentials. The time came when Ayla left the house with her parents' permission. Although it was a tough day to have, everything was worth it.

Ayla reached the hostel and settled herself down. Her roommate Jess, a charming girl, introduced herself to Lila. There was an instant bond among them. Jess was one year senior and she began to introduce every single gossip roaming. Jess took her phone and began to show the pictures of the most attractive man in fact, the lecturer Mr Knight from the English department. He was looking damn sexy in long brown boots, white pants and sweatshirt complemented by his long fur coat. The way he carried himself was just wandering, his sharp jawline with minimal beard, Romanian nose complementing his million dollar smile and glittery brown eyes were attractive enough to make any woman fall for him. Seeing the picture, Lila was totally captivated by his beauty and there was just one thing that Lila uttered,

"Charismatic!"

"Hey! Don't fall in love with this man." Jess uttered while making fun of Lila as she was blushing. He really had an impact on you Lila…..our Lila is after Mr Knight…….

Lila laughed and she punched Jess with a pillow. The night went long with laughter and tons of gossip. The alarm rang and Lila was late. She packed herself up and immediately rushed to her class. Luckily, she had Jess on her side who already helped her the fastest way to get in her class. It hardly took her five minutes to get in the class as it was 8:30 am. Lila stood by the door.

"Stand outside! Red hoodie you are late………" Mr Knight said with his aggressive tone while passing a sensual look towards Lila.

Three

An Ode to a Lover

"Note down an assignment:
Write down an ode to your favorite person, place or an object. It can be anything but make sure it should be attractive and creative."

That's all for today. See you in your next class by Wednesday along with your assignments. Professor Knight said and he began to pile up his things. He was about to leave the class as all of a sudden Lila grasped his attention. She was standing still outside of the classroom with a distress reflecting from her as she was tapping her feet against the wall. Professor noted every single tension that was rising in Lila. He packed himself up and left the class while walking a few steps apart, he turned over facing Lila and called her to come in with him.

Lila walked behind the professor with a shame that she missed her very first class. Although this was not the first day she dreamt of. Lila's face was turning pale. After a few steps, the Professor opened the door for Lila and welcomed her in. Lila stood at the one side of the cabin.

"Can I have your name?" Professor Knight said while pouring a glass of water for himself..

"I am sorry sir for being late.. I……" Lila words almost slipped down her tongue. She was figuring the right word to make a perfect fit.

"Your name!" Professor Knight said while water was running down from his throat. His wet symmetrical lips were the only reason that Lila stumbled with her words..

"Professor….its Lila Mathews……" Lila said while she immediately shifted her focus away from the professor. It was just obvious that she couldn't keep her eyes away from him.

Professor placed a piece of paper in front of her. Lila picked up the paper and this was the title of the assignment imprinted over there.

"I will be checking your assignment Miss Lila.. Make sure you represent the very best of your input…" Knight said with his sharp gaze. Lila took the paper and left the cabin immediately. Her heart was accelerating and mind was confused, questioning Lila about the dominating aura of Professor Knight.

The bell rang and Lila attended the rest of her subjects. She started working on the assignment as soon as she stepped back to her hostel room. Lila was working with all her effort on the assignment in order to win impressive grades in English literature. But poor Lila was way too innocent for the outer world. On Wednesday, Lila was on time sitting at the very front bench with her assignment placed right in front of her. Professor Knight walked in with his casual greeting. He began with the lecture introducing some methods and techniques about the literature. There was no doubt that Professor Knight was a compatible teacher at the university who had a hunch of knowledge. The way he delivered the lecture showed his passion and commitment towards his job. The time was up and Knight stepped towards Lila

"Lila! Will you please collect the assignments and submit them to my office?" Professor Knight placed a humble request in his contemporary heavy voice. Lila nodded her head and whispered a tiny yes. She followed the instructions and took the pile of assignments in Knight's cabin.

After Lila had handed over the pile of assignments to Professor Knight, he began to flip through them one by one. He then asked her to take out her assignment so that he could go over it with her personally. As Lila handed over her assignment to Professor Knight, he took a close look at it and began to point out some areas where she could improve her writing. He gave her some tips and tricks, and even shared some of his own writing techniques with her.

Professor Knight pulled up a chair next to Lila and gestured for her to sit down. She hesitated for a moment, feeling a rush of nerves as she sat down next to her handsome professor. He opened her assignment and began to read it carefully, nodding his head every so often as he scanned the pages.

"Your writing is good, Lila," he said with a smile, "but I think there's room for improvement. May I offer you some tips?"

Lila nodded eagerly, feeling grateful for his offer. Professor Knight began to point out areas where she could elaborate more, or where she could add more detail to make her writing more engaging. As he spoke, Lila found herself becoming more and more captivated by his words. She couldn't help but notice how handsome he was, with his chiseled features and deep, penetrating eyes. She tried to focus on what he was saying, but her mind kept wandering to thoughts of him. She wondered what it would be like to kiss him, to run her fingers through his thick, wavy hair. She shook her head, trying to banish the thoughts from her mind, but they kept coming back.

As the professor continued to speak, Lila felt a strange tension building between them. She couldn't quite put her finger on it, but she sensed that there was something more between them than just a student-teacher relationship. She wondered if he felt it too, or if it was all just in her imagination.

At last, the professor finished giving her feedback on her assignment. "I hope that was helpful, Lila," he said with a smile. "And please, don't hesitate to come to me if you need any more help."

Lila nodded, feeling grateful for his guidance. After spending some time discussing her assignment, Professor Knight thanked Lila for coming to see him and encouraged her to continue working hard on her writing. Lila left the office feeling inspired and grateful for the professor's guidance. As she walked back to her hostel room, Lila couldn't help but think about Professor Knight and how much she enjoyed their conversation. She wondered if there was more to their relationship than just a teacher-student dynamic. But she quickly shook off those thoughts and reminded herself of her goal - to excel in her studies and make her parents proud.

Four

A Forbidden Seedling

Knight touching her thighs sensually and growling leaning on Lila's body whispering,

"My lil angel!!!!!!!!you are…..." knight slowly mumbled Lila's skin was glowing over his hands and all she could do was breathing heavily and staring straight into Knight's eyes. Knight began to make a move straight towards her lips.

At the very moment Lila woke up as she was dragged into the daylight by Jess, her roommate..

"Jess!! This is Saturday and why why why!!!! are you waking me up?"

"Oh! My unexcited friend. ..wake up, let us see the first sunlight…… … and make a wish." Jess said with joy while dragging lila out of her sheets.

"It's 5 am in the morning and you are …pushing me….." lila said while smudging her eyes and making her vision clear.

Jess was all dressed up and she threw the jacket right in her face. Saying we are gonna get your smugly face out of the sheets. Lila whipped her face with fresh water and packed herself up. Jess dragged Lila out of the hostel room and there, sneaking out from the security guard they reached out to the mountain where the two of them were supposed to see the first sunlight. On the way. Lila was trembling as she was still in deep sleep and resetting the dream she had.

"Make a wish Lila….." Jess said while absorbing the sight of the very first sunlight.

Make him mine….Lila whispered. Jess narrowed down a sharp stare at her.

"Wait! Who? Jess questioned

"Your boyfriend.." Lila laughed and told her that she did not believe in these stupid things.

"Well! I can prove. I hope that Lila finds her soulmate at college…." Jess said while facing towards the sun and aligning her hands.

"Who is this? Mr Knight!! Lila threw a laugh…."

"Don't you think of that man Lila . He is not the right one and while standing here don't utter that nonsense." Jess said with a damn serious tone.

Lila smiled and stepped back as she knew that Jess was not in the mood of hearing her out. Lila was so sleepy that her eyes could not stand there. She asked Jess to get back to the hostel room. Jess told her that she is free to go. Lila stumbled back taking a short morning walk back to her room. Lila woke up and found Jess holding her phone and narrowing an aggressive gaze at her.

"Are you and Knight dating? Is he messing with you? Tell me Lila…" Jess yelled at her.

"Oh wait! Wait why Jess. What is this?" Lila asked her.

Jess turned the phone screen on and there was an anonymous intimate message. Jess read out that loud. The message says that Knight is asking Lila to come over at lunch.

"What the hell are you trying to do, Lila. I warned you already. What are you doing girl?" Jess was so mad.

Lila sat on her bed, her face full of confusion and concern as Jess paced around the room, telling her the story of a girl who had fallen for Professor Knight.

"This girl, she was just like you, Lila. So innocent and full of life. She thought Professor Knight was the one for her, and he seemed to feel the same way. They started dating, and she was so happy," Jess explained, her voice filled with sadness.

"But then, one day, he just stopped answering her calls. She tried to talk to him, but he ignored her completely. And then, she found out that he had been seeing someone else the whole time. She was devastated, Lila. It took her months to get over him, and even then, she was never the same."

Lila listened to Jess's story, her heart heavy with empathy for the girl who had been hurt. She couldn't imagine going through something like that herself. Lila was shocked and didn't know how to react. She couldn't believe that someone would spread such rumors about her and Knight. She quickly grabbed the phone from Jess's hand and tried to explain the situation.

"Jess, this is not what it looks like. I am not dating Professor Knight, and he hasn't made any advances towards me. This message must be a prank or a mistake," Lila said, trying to convince her friend.

But Jess was not convinced. She had heard stories about Knight and how he had broken the hearts of several girls on campus. She told Lila about a young girl who had fallen in love with Knight and how he had toyed with her emotions before breaking her heart.

"Lila, you need to stay away from him. I don't want to see you get hurt like that poor girl," Jess warned her.

Lila listened to Jess's story with a heavy heart. She had always admired Professor Knight and his passion for literature. She had hoped to learn more from him and improve her writing skills. But now, she wasn't sure if she could trust him.

"I understand your concern, Jess, but I am not interested in Professor Knight in that way. I just want to learn from him and improve my writing skills," Lila said, trying to assure her friend.

Jess looked at Lila for a moment and then sighed. "Okay, I trust you. But please be careful, Lila. Don't let your admiration for him blind you to his true intentions."

As Jess told her the story, Lila couldn't help but feel conflicted. On one hand, she was attracted to Professor Knight and was curious about the message he sent her. But on the other hand, she didn't want to make the same mistake as the girl in Jess's story and end up heartbroken.

Lila's mind was racing with thoughts and emotions. She didn't know what to do. She wanted to believe that Knight was sincere in his interest in her and that he wasn't like the person Jess described, but she couldn't shake the feeling of doubt.

She knew that Jess had her best interests at heart, but she couldn't ignore the pull she felt towards Knight. She decided that she needed to be cautious and not let herself get too involved too quickly. After a few moments of silence, Lila finally spoke up.

"Jess, I hear what you're saying and I appreciate your concern. But I need to figure things out for myself. I can't just avoid someone just because of what someone else went through. I'm not saying that I'm going to pursue anything with Professor Knight, but I also don't want to ignore what I feel."

Jess sighed but nodded in understanding. "Okay, Lila. Just promise me that you'll be careful and not get too invested too quickly. And if he does anything to hurt you, you'll come to me and we'll figure it out together." Lila smiled and hugged Jess.

"Thank you for looking out for me, Jess. I promise I'll be careful."

Five

Veto Kiss

For days, Jess' confession towards the hypocritical narcissistic Knight's personality was roaming over her mind. Lila took hostage among those thoughts, and she did not even pay a single reply to the professor. During the weekend, Lila went straight to her parents as promised. She spent the next two days without looking at her phone. She managed to give her every single moment to her parents. Ayla, Levin, and Lila cooked together, went on a short bicycle trip in the countryside and even on Sunday they did have a picnic right before Lila was leaving. She paid a goodbye to her parents and took the last subway that follows the route back to her college. She landed in her hostel room sharp at 9 pm. There was a usual crowd at the hostel, like her many hostel mates were getting themselves assembled for the college. Lila walked down the hallway carrying her luggage. Surprisingly, the door was locked.

It could only mean one thing that Jess might not be there. Lila took her phone out from her right pocket and began to dial Jess. Her one hand was on the knob and the other one was on the phone. As Lila was dialing Jess, Lila heard heavy footsteps approaching her. She turned to see and there was Professor Knight standing up in his long black boots complemented by high neck jeans and long brown coat. He was wearing a cap that almost made him look camouflage.

"Oh professor, you scared me!" Lila said while holding herself. She was having an accelerated heartbeat with her pupils all dilated.

"Lila!…" Professor said while looking deep in her eyes. He took Lila's phone from her and opened up the messenger and showed the screen right in front of her face.

"Um! professor I was busy therefore I couldn't reply the texts." Lila said with her shivering tone.

Knight leaned on her, grabbed her right hand and handed her over her cell phone while stepping one step closer to her. He leaned on poor Lila and whispered slowly,

"I am seeing you the very first thing in the morning. Pack yourself as I won't restrain myself from paying you another visit.." Knight said with his presiding tone. Lila could smell his breath; his warm breath was strong enough to turn Lila's blood cold. She hardly took a breath.

Professor took one step back and it seemed that he immediately vanished in the air. Lila was standing still like a statue. In the meantime, Jess walked up to her and asked Lila what happened. Lila was in shock about what the professor wanted from her. Lila made an obsolete excuse to cover up the whole matter. Jess took her keys out and opened the door for her. Jess was all up there telling Lila every bit of detail about her weekend. But Lila was in her deep thoughts trying to figure out the matter. That night, Lila stayed up all night trying to answer Mr knight's approach towards her. His intentions were clear that he is attracted to her but at the same time, Jess's words cross her disarray thoughts warning her to abstain from him. The only way to find out the real intention of the professor was to confront him as his words were still incarnated in her mind.

The next morning, Lila skipped Mr. Knight's class and went straight to his cabin waiting for him. Professor walked in and seeing Lila there was a strange aggressive smile.

"Come in Miss Lila!" Professor said while opening the door.

As Lila stepped into Mr. Knight's cabin, she was met with a warm smile. Knight gestured for her to take a seat and began discussing the English literature lesson she had missed. He explained the themes and motifs of the text with such passion that Lila found herself engrossed in the discussion. She felt a sense of ease and comfort around Knight, and for a moment, she forgot all her worries. As Lila sat down, Knight gestured to a bookshelf and asked,

"Have you read any of these works yet?" Lila shook her head, feeling a bit embarrassed at her lack of familiarity with the classics. Knight picked out a volume of Shakespeare's sonnets and opened it to a random page.

"Let's start with this one," he said, pointing to Sonnet 18. "Have you heard the phrase 'Shall I compare thee to a summer's day?' before?"

Lila nodded, recognizing the line. Knight then launched into an enthusiastic explanation of the poem's structure, language, and themes, using examples from other sonnets to illustrate his points. He talked about the use of iambic pentameter, the extended metaphor of the speaker's beloved as a "temperate" day, and the contrast between the fickleness of nature and the constancy of love. As Knight spoke, Lila found herself drawn in by his passion for the subject and his ability to make even complex concepts understandable. She asked questions and shared her own interpretations, feeling like she was learning more in this one-on-one session than she ever had in a lecture. Knight's enthusiasm was contagious, and soon Lila found herself participating in the discussion with equal fervor. They delved into the nuances of the text, analyzing the characters and their motivations. It was a refreshing change from the monotony of regular classes.

As the lesson ended, Knight leaned back in his chair and looked at Lila with a twinkle in his eye. "You have a real knack for literature, Miss Lila. I can see that you have a natural talent for it."

Lila blushed, feeling a sense of pride at Knight's words. She had always been passionate about literature, but never had someone acknowledged her talent before. As she gathered her things to leave, Knight walked her to the door. Just as she was about to step out, he leaned in and placed a gentle kiss on her cheek. Both felt butterflies in the stomach and sensual feelings were streaming down in their body. He leaned towards her, grabbed her from her back slowly while ruffling her hair. He looked towards her and he kissed her gently.

"I look forward to our next lesson, Miss Lila," he whispered. Lila felt a flutter in her stomach as she stepped out of the cabin. She couldn't deny the attraction she felt towards Knight, but Jess's words continued to haunt her. She knew she had to tread carefully, but for now, she was content to enjoy the literature lessons and the company of her charming professor.

Six

A Secret Relationship

A bright summer day, it was lunchtime and today there was an unusual chatter of students and the faculty. The summer season festival had just started, there were tons of attractive stalls all piled up with tons of food items artifacts and even clothing that were perfect to design the summer outlet. Lila was up there visiting stalls grabbing the view. All of a sudden the professor caught her eye, he was surrounded by some chicks from the college. The girls who looked even hotter than her. She stood by the long alignment of stalls and drew a suspicious eye on them. The girls were offering the professor some drinks making a strong eye contact. All of a sudden, Knight caught her and he passed down an intimate smile at Lila. Lila hid herself up to the very best as she did not want professor knight to think that she was ghosting him right after the last kiss they shared. Lila walked down the narrow hallway to get a little escape, meanwhile she was immediately dragged into one of the cold storage rooms.

Breathe! Lila…. Knight whispered in her ears while covering her face with the right hand and grabbing her tiny waist with his left one.

It was cold and dark with a tiny window throwing sunlight in bits and pieces. He removed his hands from Lila's mouth and began to cuddle her face by running his fingers all over her cheeks down her neck. Lila's heart skipped a beat but she remembers that a few minutes ago how recklessly knight was flirting with some of the hottest chicks of the college. Blood rushed through her veins and her cheeks turned bright red. She began to throw knights hands off from her but he was holding her firm looking at her neckline that extends straight to her breasts.

"What the hell are you trying to do?" Lila asked with a rush of anger throbbing her lips.

"Oh! It smells like jealousy……" Knight said while grabbing her closer. Their bodies were touching one another and Lila could feel even the sharp clutch of Knight's waistband. Lila looked in his eyes with all her aggression. Meanwhile, Knight leaned on her and whispered,

"Watch your tone my Lil Angel! I know you are getting off the road." He growls while sliding down his one hand in Lila's thighs.

"What does that kiss mean to you?" Lila asked while she felt strong sensations running down her body. Knight slipped his fingers in her and began to grab her with his sensual touch and threw her against the wall while giving her soft sensual pleasure.

"You mean so much to me Lila. I can't and I won't restrain myself from you." Knight said and he began to kiss her lips gently. Their lips were gliding over one another. At that very moment, Knight heard some heavy steps approaching the room. He stopped and dragged Lila to one of the old caskets.

Lila was there all in his hands calculating what just happened in there while Mr. Knight made a sharp move to save the two of them. Lila was sitting beside him just like a little baby who snuggles. Her anger was blown away and now she was calm.

"Lila! I want to see you at my apartment tonight. But right now, gather yourself up and get back to the festival."

Seven

A Bearable Loss

S nuggling under the sheets, Lila caresses against the purple illusionist sheets that were all scattered on Knight's bed. It was an incredible night. They made love several times until the morning goose clucked in. The sun was up and the day was about to get kicked in. Lila was still in bed and Knight was there sitting on a couch placed at the very corner of the room. A towel twisted around his thick waist highlighting Knight's abs were just implicit. Lila woke up and saw that Knight was lying next to her in towel. He smells fresh just like a spring bath has walked on the bed.

"Good morning Pie!" He said while moving Lila's hair strands away from her pretty face.

"Good morning Professor!!" Lila said while laughing. Knight smiled at her face and grabbed her by saying,

"Wasn't last night enough to make the two of us clear about our relationship….." Knight questioned her while staring intensely at Lila's body.

"Oh! I forged another lesson or a group of lessons will be enough to teach this grumpy student…." Lila said and threw a smile.

"Get up Lila. We do have so much to do today." He said while laying back on bed.

"Breakfast is ready Lila. Come join me…" he said while getting up from bed and heading straight to the living area where breakfast was already assembled. Lila wore her clothes and looked at her phone. There were more than ten missed calls from Jess and her mother. She picked herself up and left Knight's apartment in a hurry.

It was the fifth time Lila missed her class. She opened up the texts and there was just one thing saying "call me"! Lila called Jess first and asked what's the matter. She told her that her batch coordinator connected with Lila's mother and informed her that Lila has been missing many classes per week. Lila hung up the phone and now was thinking about how to answer her mother. Instead of calling her mother, Lila went straight to the campus and attended the rest of her class. She went straight to the coordinator's room who had placed a call to her mother.

"May I take a few minutes sir?" Lila asked

The person sitting in the chair turned over and surprisingly this was a quite familiar face. This was professor knight.

"What does your ruthless act mean? What are you trying to do?" Lila asked while punching down the table sharply.

Watch your tone miss Lila, you are standing in front of your coordinator and professor. I want you to go through your grades. Knight said and handed her a piece of paper where all the supporting information was there. And he continued.

"Your grades have been dropping and I am worried that if things continue like this, we have to withdraw your scholarship." Professor said and asked Lila to leave.

"Dumbass!…what does he want from me? " Lila said while leaving the campus. When she got back to her room, Jess was waiting for her, looking worried.

"Lila, Ayla, your mother asked me about you today," Jess said, her voice low.

"What did she ask?" Lila asked, feeling a sense of dread.

"She asked if you were seeing anyone, and if you were involved with Professor Knight,. I think someone told her something," Jess said, watching Lila's reaction closely.

Lila's heart sank at the mention of Knight's name. She knew that if Ayla was asking about her relationship status, it meant that word had gotten around about her and Knight. "What did you tell her?" Lila asked, trying to keep her voice steady.

"I told her that you and Knight are just friends, but she seemed skeptical," Jess said, frowning. "Lila, I need to know the truth. Are you involved with him?" Lila hesitated, not sure how to answer. She knew that Jess wouldn't approve of her relationship with Knight, but she also couldn't deny the feelings she had for him. Finally, she spoke the truth.

"Yes, Jess. I am involved with him." Jess's face fell, and Lila could see the disappointment and concern written all over her features.

"Lila, I don't know what to say. You know how I feel about this. Knight is your professor, and he could get in serious trouble if anyone found out about your relationship."

"I know, Jess. Believe me, I never planned for any of this to happen," Lila said, feeling tears prick at the corners of her eyes. "But I can't help the way I feel. And I don't want to hide my relationship with Knight."

Jess sighed and put a hand on Lila's shoulder. "I understand that, Lila. But you have to be careful. This could all blow up in your face. And what about after the semester ends? Are you going to keep seeing him?" Lila shook her head, feeling overwhelmed. She didn't have all the answers, but she knew that she couldn't just walk away from her feelings for Knight.

"I don't know, Jess. I really don't. But for now, I just need to figure out how to navigate this situation." Jess nodded, still looking worried. "Okay, Lila. But promise me you'll be careful. And if you need anything, I'm here for you."

Eight

A Subtle Change

"It's been the third weekend that Lila has not visited us," Ayla said with a lower tone. She was sad and at the same time angry and missing her daughter too much. Every single weekend when she calls her, Lila always comes up with an excuse that she is working on her grades. The only thing that comforted Ayla was that her daughter is studying quite hard to get good grades. Apparently, that was what was being portrayed to Lila's parents, meanwhile Lila struggled to manage her secretive relationship with professor knight and her studies. But little did Ayla know that those weekends were not being spent in the name of getting some good grades, instead Lila was making her way to professor knight and staying with him. Chilling like any other ordinary couple. Despite the considerable age difference everything was running smooth, but little did they know that they will soon confront some obstacles. Knight and Lila were enjoying their romanticism and sexualities regardless of risks their relationship imposed. For instance, Lila and Knight were making their best efforts to cover up their relationship status at the college as this was clearly against the college principles that a teacher must not be in any romantic relationship with a student. Lila was scared of what her parents will think if they get to find out.

Ayla asked Levin if they could pay a visit to their daughter as she has been working very hard in school. Levin did agree and the two of them took the very first road trip straight to Lila's hostel. After 45 minutes of driving straight to Lila's place, Ayla knocked at the door, surprisingly Jess walked out, and she was shocked.

"Is Lila there?" Ayla asked Jess while Jess was looking straight at the two of them.

"Ummm…she was here just before you arrived. I will call her, please wait here…" Jess tried to cover up for her friend, but little did she know that Ayla had already caught her.

Jess took her phone and called Lila asking her to come back to the hostel as her parents are there. Lila told Jess to make up an excuse that will send her parents back home. Lila's statement triggered Jess' aggression, and she yelled at her asking her to stop dating Mr. Knight.

"He is not the right man. You are playing with fire Lila…".Jess said meanwhile she thought she heard footsteps behind her. Jess turned and saw Lila's mother listening to her conversation.

"Miss Ayla. I can explain." Jess said while hanging up the phone. Her words stuttered.

"You are not the one doing the explanation." Call Lila and tell her to get herself at the school's cafe. Her father and I will be waiting for her. Ayla said and she left with her husband. Jess called Lila and spilled the beans as she knew that it was going to be hell for Lila.

Nine

A Dreadful Reveal

"I am in love with him. mother!" Lila said with half teary eyes…

"You can't be…" Ayla scolded with an aggression that propelled straight from her eyes..

All of a sudden Lila woke up saying what a terrible nightmare and took a glass of water next to her to quench her thirst.

"Well! You are a living nightmare…" Knight whispered while kissing her neck gently..

"Hey! I need to get up…" Lila said while pushing his hands off from her body.

"I think we should get a break……" Lila said while tucking her skirts in.

"Oh! Lila, don't be ridiculous. there is no one and nothing is going to happen to us. As long as I am here. Knight said while he gently creases her cheeks. Lila smiled and left the room. She attended college just like her regular days. On the other hand, things between her and her parents were all heated up. After getting a final warning from them Lila was still having hope to convince her parents. Regardless, Lila and

Mr. Knight are recklessly enjoying themselves, till one day the actual danger knocks at their door.

Like the usual days, Lila was attending the classes and one of the representatives from the board office entered the class. He was a tall guy with a broad figure approximately in his middle age around 35 or 40 years. He was black with no hair at all wearing a loose pants with tucked in shorts. There was a batch on his right chest that said his name, although it was of dark blue color clearly identifying that he is the member of higher education regulation authority, the ones who manages discipline and ensures the safety of other students including the faculty. He stood by the entrance and called loudly a very familiar name.

"Miss Lila…" he said and stared straight towards Lila. He was a cold guy in fact with no smile at all.

Lila stood up with a question on her face, although she was doing great on her grades, at least they were satisfactory enough to regulate her scholarship for the near future.

"Come with me, Miss Lila…" the well-suited man said and began to lead her straight to the board roam. Lila read the name of the batch, this was Richy Morry.

"Mr Richy! Is everything alright?" Lila asked with a hesitation.

"You will find this soon.." Richy answered.

He opened the door and found that Professor Knight along with the other college officials were waiting for her. She acted in a very normal way, there was a surprise on her face and fear inside. Lila was shaking but she gracefully greeted them. One of the members asked Lila to make herself comfortable in the chair. She did and was looking at them. She saw that Professor Knight was sitting up with all his confidence so everything would be alright. While making tons of questions in her mind one of the members introduced herself as Laura Rachelle. She was a bit of a young lady and told the two of them that the board has some questions for them. At every moment, there was a short memory that glanced in Lila's mind. Mr. Knight asked her that if there is any member to question you about anything simply deny them all, and the rest of the matter will be taken care of by him.

The session began!

Rachelle cleared her throat and looked directly at Lila. "Miss Lila, we have received some information regarding your relationship with Professor Knight. Can you confirm or deny this?" Lila's heart raced as she tried to come up with a plausible answer. She looked at Knight, who gave her a reassuring nod. Taking a deep breath, Lila responded,

"I'm sorry, but I cannot confirm any such relationship. Professor Knight is my teacher and I have the utmost respect for him in that capacity. However, there is nothing more between us."

Laura looked at her skeptically, but Knight spoke up. "Miss Rachelle, I can assure you that there is no inappropriate relationship between me and Miss Lila. As her professor, I have a duty to ensure that she receives the best education possible, and that is all that our interactions have been about."

The other board members nodded in agreement, and Laura seemed satisfied with the response. "Very well, we will take your word for it, Professor Knight. Miss Lila, you are free to go and resume your studies. We apologize for any inconvenience."

Lila let out a sigh of relief as she gathered her things and left the room. As she walked down the hall, she couldn't help but feel a sense of guilt for lying to the board. However, she knew that it was the only way to protect herself and Knight from any potential consequences.

After the session, Lila was allowed to go back to her class, but she couldn't concentrate on anything. She kept thinking about the questions and the situation she was in. She was grateful that Knight had handled everything smoothly, but at the same time, she was worried about what the board members thought of her.

When she finally saw Knight in class, he gave her a reassuring smile, which made her feel a little better. She knew that she could trust him, and that he would always have her back.

Ten

A Dreadful End

"I have taken care of everything, since we are under Rachelle's radar, we should drop our meetings for a while…" knight!

The notification popped up on Lila's phone and hearing words from him made her comfortable. She could finally breathe in as Lila won't afford any loss. She was struggling with her grades, her best friend Jess' reckless attitude and her parent's disapproval and for now she was constantly overlooked by Rachelle. The saddest part of all was that Knight and Lila did not intend to meet as they knew that if they crossed the line this one more time things would heat up. Lila observed on her own that Rachelle was watching her every move while she was at the campus. That hide and seek game was irritating and by now everything turned out to be quite annoying for her. Things even got worse, when Lila found that someone at the hostel is assisting Rachelle. Rachelle's spy heard the staff talking over Lila and Knight's secret relationship. Rachelle's spy started digging and asking more questions till she discovered everything was true..

Lila and knight were staying away from each other on purpose, and they had not seen each other for the past two weeks. Lila missed him a lot and expected that Knight will be feeling the same. But she was quite wrong in assuming things. The college held an annual robotics gala where every class was supposed to come up with their projects. Lila attended the fair just to encourage her best friend Jess. While Lila was roaming, looking and appreciating everyone on their hard work and how beautifully they all have illustrated the idea. Then something just grabbed her attention, there was a woman standing beside professor knight. Her head was covered with a scarf and she almost disguised herself with a pair of sunglasses and a leather jacket complimenting her flary lilies dress. Lila stood by there and began to watch, she sounded a bit tensed. Knight comforted her and took that woman in his cabin.

The whole thing was really pissing Lila off. She secretly followed the two of them. Instead of getting into the cabin, Mr. knight brought her to the very same room where Lila and he used to meet and make love. She followed and stood by the door hearing all the conversation. She stood by and heard them talking over their past relationship, the girl was yelling at him how terribly she missed him and how she wanted to get back in a relationship with him.

Lila ran into them and found out that Mr. knight was there just like they used to get in there. Seeing Lila, Mr. knight stepped back and began to rectify his situation.

"I can explain!! Knight whispered…" but Lila was in no mood to accept an explanation, she dragged the girl out of the room and began to yell at Knight's face.

"Why the hell would you do this? A damn cheater!" Lila yelled with all her throat.

"How could you?!" she screamed at him, her voice shaking with emotion. "You're a damn cheater!"

Knight tried to explain, but Lila wasn't in the mood to listen. She pushed him away when he stepped forward, and things only got worse when Rachelle entered the room.

Lila turned back to Knight, tears streaming down her face. "I can't do this anymore. We're through." And with that, she stormed out of the room, never looking back.

As Lila left the room, her emotions were overwhelming. She felt betrayed, hurt, and ashamed that she had let herself fall for Knight's charm. She walked out of the building and into the open air, trying to calm herself down. Lila had always been a strong and independent woman, but in that moment, she felt vulnerable and alone. She couldn't believe she had let herself be fooled by Knight's sweet words and gentle touches.

As she walked, her thoughts were a jumbled mess. She wondered how she could have been so blind to his true intentions, and how she could have been so foolish to believe that he cared about her. She felt used and manipulated. Despite the pain she was feeling, Lila was determined not to let Knight's actions define her. She knew that she had to pick herself up and move forward, even if it meant doing so alone. She would not allow herself to be vulnerable to such a man again.

With a deep breath, Lila pushed her emotions aside and focused on her future. She knew that she had a bright one ahead of her, and that she would not let anyone, especially a man like Knight, bring her down.

Eleven

A Fresh Start

Just like the dried autumn days. Lila's heart was quenching and feeding her soul with pain. Lila almost risked everything in that relationship. Lila sat in her room, staring blankly at the wall in front of her. It had been weeks since she ended things with Mr. Knight, but she couldn't shake the feeling of emptiness that seemed to consume her. She had tried everything to move on - hanging out with friends, diving into her studies, even going on dates with other guys - but nothing seemed to work. She couldn't stop thinking about him, about the moments they had shared together, about the way his eyes lit up when he talked about his passion for English literature.

Lila started to question whether their love was real. Had Mr. Knight been playing her all along? Had he used his position of power to manipulate her? The thought of it made her sick to her stomach, but she couldn't help but wonder.

As she lay in bed one night, Lila found herself scrolling through old messages between her and Mr. Knight. She read over the sweet nothings he used to whisper to her and the promises he made. It all seemed so genuine at the time, but now she couldn't help but wonder if it was all just an act.

But then she remembered the way he used to look at her - with such love and adoration in his eyes. The way he used to hold her close and tell her how much he cared for her. Could all of that have been fake? Lila couldn't bear the thought of it.

As the weeks turned into months, Lila tried her best to move on. She started to distance herself from Mr. Knight and began focusing on her own life. But no matter how hard she tried, she couldn't stop thinking about him. The memories of their time together kept flooding back to her, and she couldn't shake the feeling that what they had shared was real. One night, as she lay in bed, Lila realized that she was still in love with Mr. Knight. She knew that it was wrong, that she should be moving on, but she couldn't help the way she felt. She had never felt such a strong connection with anyone before, and she couldn't imagine ever feeling that way again.

Lila knew that she needed to come to terms with her feelings and figure out how to move on. But for now, she allowed herself to indulge in her memories of Mr. Knight and the love that they had shared.

Lila walked into the university campus, her eyes scanning the crowds of students, trying to avoid any familiar faces. As she made her way towards the lecture hall, she couldn't help but feel a sinking feeling in her stomach. She knew it was only a matter of time before she saw him again.

As she entered the lecture hall, she tried to keep her head down, not wanting to draw any attention to herself. She found a seat towards the back, hoping to blend in with the rest of the students. But as she looked up, she saw him. Professor Knight was standing at the front of the lecture hall, his eyes scanning the room. Lila's heart skipped a beat. She could feel the heat rising in her cheeks as she tried to avoid his gaze.

She couldn't believe how much of an effect he still had on her, despite everything that had happened.

As the lecture began, Lila tried to focus on the material, but her mind kept wandering back to him. She couldn't help but think about their time together, the way he made her feel, and the memories they shared. But as much as she wanted to hold onto those memories, she knew that it was time to move on.

She tried to ignore him, to act as if he wasn't even in the room, but every time he spoke, her ears perked up, and her heart raced. She could feel the pull towards him, the desire to be near him again, but she knew that she had to resist.

The lecture finally came to an end, and as the students began to file out of the room, Lila sat frozen in her seat, watching as he made his way towards the door. She could feel her heart pounding in her chest as she tried to figure out what to do next.

As he walked by her seat, she could feel the electricity between them, the tension that still lingered from their past. But as much as she wanted to reach out and touch him, to tell him how she felt, she knew that she had to keep her distance. She watched as he walked out of the room, disappearing from her sight. A part of her wanted to run after him, to tell him everything, but she knew that it was too late. The damage had been done, and there was no going back.

As she gathered her things and made her way out of the lecture hall, she knew that it was time to let go. She couldn't keep living in the past, holding onto something that was no longer there. It was time to move on, to start a new chapter in her life, and to leave Mr. Knight behind.

Twelve

Unanticipated support

s Lila tried to move on from her relationship with Mr. Knight, her friend Jess continued to be a constant support for her. She knew that Lila was going through a tough time and decided to take her out for dinner.

"Come on Lila, let's go out for dinner tonight. You've been cooped up in your apartment for too long," Jess said, trying to cheer her up. Lila hesitated at first, but eventually agreed. They went to one of their favorite restaurants and sat down at a cozy corner table.

"Thanks for doing this Jess," Lila said, smiling weakly.

"Of course, girl. Anything for you," Jess replied, returning the smile. They ordered their food and started talking about random things. Jess made sure to keep the conversation light and easy. However, Lila couldn't help but think about Mr. Knight. She wondered if he was thinking about her too. Suddenly, her thoughts were interrupted by Jess's voice.

"Lila, you know that you deserve better, right?"

Lila looked at her friend, confused.

"What do you mean?" she asked.

"I mean that Mr. Knight was never good enough for you. He may have been charming and intelligent, but he treated you badly. You deserve someone who will treat you with respect and love you for who you are," Jess explained.

Lila nodded, realizing that Jess was right. She had been so caught up in her feelings for Mr. Knight that she had forgotten her worth. She knew that she needed to move on and find someone who would love and cherish her.

As they finished their meal, Lila felt a sense of relief. She knew that she had a long way to go, but having Jess by her side made the journey a little easier.

"Thank you for tonight, Jess. I really needed this," Lila said, smiling gratefully.

"Anytime, girl. I'm always here for you," Jess replied, returning the smile. As they walked out of the restaurant, Lila felt a sense of hope. She knew that it wouldn't be easy, but she was determined to move on and find happiness.

As they finished their dinner, Jess suggested to Lila, "You know, my parents are in town this weekend. I think it would be great if we could visit them. Get away from the city for a bit and just relax."

Lila wasn't sure if she was up for it, but she knew she needed a break from her routine. "I don't know, Jess. I don't want to be a burden."

"You're not a burden, Lila. My parents would be more than happy to have you over. Plus, it would be great for you to get out of your head for a bit." Lila hesitated for a moment before finally agreeing.

"Okay, let's do it."

The next day, they packed their bags and drove to Jess's parents' house. As they arrived, Jess's parents welcomed them with open arms. They spent the day exploring the town and having a relaxing time. That evening, as they were sitting on the porch enjoying the sunset, Jess's mother asked Lila how she was doing.

Lila didn't want to burden Jess's parents with her problems, but Jess's mother insisted, "You can talk to us, Lila. We're here for you."

Lila opened up about her recent breakup with Mr. Knight and how it was affecting her. She felt foolish for falling for him, and she was having a hard time moving on.

Jess's mother listened patiently and then offered some words of wisdom. "Lila, you're not foolish for falling in love. It happens to everyone. And it's okay to take some time to heal. Just don't let this experience make you lose hope in love."

Lila took her words to heart and felt grateful for having such a supportive friend and family. She knew that moving on would take time, but she felt more hopeful about the future.

After that Jess' mother took them to a nearby park, which was surrounded by lush green trees and a sparkling lake in the middle. The cool breeze was blowing, and the sun was shining brightly, making everything look picture-perfect. Lila was lost in her thoughts, but the beauty of nature managed to soothe her mind. She watched children playing and laughing, and the sight brought a smile to her face.

As they walked, they stumbled upon a small lake, where they saw ducks and swans swimming. Jess's mother suggested that they should feed them, and she bought a bag of bread crumbs from a vendor. Lila and Jess were overjoyed, and they ran towards the lake. The ducks and swans quacked and honked as they saw them approaching. They could hardly contain their excitement. Lila's mother and Jess started to feed them, and Lila was amazed by the beauty of these birds. They were graceful, elegant, and regal. It was as if they were royalty, and the lake was their kingdom. As they were feeding the birds, Jess's mother started to tell stories from her childhood. She talked about her school days, her friends, and the pranks they used to play. Lila listened intently, and for a brief moment, she forgot about all her worries.

After they finished feeding the birds, they sat on a bench and watched the sun go down. The sky was a mixture of orange, pink, and purple, and it looked like a painting. Lila felt a sense of calmness wash over her. She realized that she was fortunate to have such a caring Jess's mother and a loyal friend like Jess. As they were leaving the park, Jess hugged her and told her that everything would be alright. Jess put her arm around Lila's shoulder and said, "We're here for you, no matter what." Lila felt grateful, and for the first time in a while, she felt like she could move on from her past and start anew.

Both of them had fun and now finally they headed back towards the hostel and started pursuing their studies. Meanwhile, Lila found a true sense of purpose in her life.

As Lila threw herself into her studies, her grades began to improve. She spent most of her days at the library, pouring over books and taking diligent notes. She found that her mind was clearer when she was focused on her studies, and it helped her to forget about the pain of her past relationship.

As she worked hard on her studies, Lila also began to explore her creativity again. She had always loved writing, but she had not written anything in a long time. One day, she decided to sit down and start writing a novel. It was a story about a young woman who had just gone through a heartbreak and was struggling to find her way in the world. Lila poured all of her emotions into the novel, and it helped her to process the pain that she had been feeling. As she wrote, she found that her words flowed easily, and she was able to create a story that was both moving and heartfelt. She continued to work on her novel every day, and she found that it gave her a sense of purpose and direction. She had always been a dreamer, but now she had something concrete to work towards. Her novel was a way for her to express herself and to share her story with the world.

As Lila worked on her novel, she also focused on her studies. She had always been a good student, but now she was determined to excel. She spent long hours in the library, reading and studying, and she was rewarded with top grades in all of her classes. With each passing day, Lila felt more and more confident in herself. She had found a new sense of purpose and direction, and she was determined to make the most of it. Her writing had given her a way to express her emotions and to work through her pain, and her studies had given her a way to focus her mind and to achieve her goals.

As Lila continued to write her novel and to excel in her studies, she realized that she had come a long way from the brokenhearted girl that she had been just a few months ago. She was stronger now, more resilient, and more determined than ever to succeed. And as she looked towards the future, she knew that anything was possible.

Thirteen

Drudgery

Lila had always been a vivid dreamer, but one night, a dream came to her that felt different than any other she had experienced before.

In the dream, she found herself walking through a dense forest with a small notebook in her hand. As she walked, she noticed that the trees around her were pulsing with an otherworldly energy, and she felt a deep sense of connection to them.

As she continued down the path, she saw a clearing up ahead. As she entered the clearing, she noticed that there was a small cabin in the center. She felt drawn to it and approached the door. When she opened the door, she found herself in a cozy room with a fireplace crackling in the corner. In the center of the room was a large wooden table covered in blank pages, quills, and inkwells. Lila felt an urge to write, so she sat down at the table and began to scribble her thoughts onto the blank pages. As she wrote, she felt a sense of release and clarity that she had never experienced before. Suddenly, a figure appeared in the doorway of the cabin. It was an old woman with kind eyes and a gentle smile.

She approached Lila and placed a hand on her shoulder.

"My dear," the old woman said, "You have a gift for writing. Your words have the power to heal and transform, both for yourself and for others. Keep writing, my dear, and you will find your way."

Lila woke up from the dream feeling invigorated and inspired. She felt as though the dream was a sign that she needed to start writing again, not just in her journal, but in a more meaningful way. She decided then and there that she would begin working on her own novel, a story that would capture the emotions and experiences that had been swirling around inside her for so long.

She began to write about everything she was feeling - the hurt, the betrayal, the confusion, and the anger. As she typed away, it was like a weight had been lifted off of her shoulders. She wrote about her relationship with Mr. Knight, how it had made her feel, and how it had ultimately ended in heartbreak. Writing was therapeutic for her, and she poured out all of her emotions onto the page.

As she wrote, she realized that she had been neglecting her studies and her writing for too long. She had been so consumed with her relationship that she had forgotten about her own dreams and ambitions. But now, she felt a newfound sense of purpose. Lila decided to start working on her own novel. She spent hours each day writing, pouring her heart and soul into the story. It was a story about a young woman who had been through a difficult breakup and was trying to find her way back to herself. Lila drew on her own experiences to create a powerful and emotional story that would touch the hearts of readers. Some snippets of poetry that Lila wrote in her journal:

"Love, a fickle flame that flickers and fades,
Leaving behind only embers and shades.
Passion and pain, a dance of two
A tale as old as time, but always new."
"Heartbreak, a storm that rages within,

A tempest of tears that never ends.

A shattered soul, a broken heart"

As she worked on her novel, Lila continued to write in her journal. She wrote about her progress with her writing, her studies, and her personal growth. She wrote about the ups and downs of her emotions, and how she was learning to deal with them in healthy ways. The more she wrote, the more she realized how important it was to express herself and share her story with others. She began to see the power of her words, and how they could inspire and help others who were going through similar struggles. Lila's journal became a place of healing and growth for her, and she continued to write in it every day. She knew that it was through her writing that she could find her voice and share her story with the world. And with each passing day, she felt stronger, more confident, and more determined to succeed.

The day of Lila's convocation had arrived. She had worked hard for this moment and was excited to receive her degree. She arrived at the venue, wearing a beautiful gown and a cap, with her family and friends. She felt proud of herself, and her mother's eyes were filled with tears of joy. As Lila walked towards the stage, she saw Professor Knight sitting in the audience. It had been a while since she last saw him, and she felt a pang in her heart. She quickly composed herself, knowing that this was her day, and nothing could ruin it. When her name was called, Lila walked up to the stage, and the dean handed her the degree. She felt a sense of accomplishment as she looked out into the crowd, seeing her family and friends cheering for her. She felt a sense of relief that all the hard work had paid off.

After the ceremony, Lila's family and friends congratulated her and took many pictures with her. She felt grateful for the support they had given her throughout her academic journey. Her mother took her aside and said,

"I am so proud of you, my dear. You have come a long way." Lila smiled and hugged her mother, feeling happy and content. She had finally accomplished her dream, and nothing could take that away from her. She looked out into the crowd and saw Professor Knight leaving the venue. She felt a sense of closure, knowing that she was moving forward, and the past was behind her.

Fourteen

New swing

The party was in full swing as Ayla and Levin hosted a celebration for Lila's graduation. The house was decorated with balloons and streamers, and there was a buffet table set up with all kinds of delicious food. Lila's friends and family were all gathered together, congratulating her on her achievement and wishing her well for the future. Lila wore a stunning emerald green dress that hugged her curves in all the right places. The dress had a low V-neckline and a flowy skirt that brushed against her ankles as she walked. She had paired it with silver heels that added a touch of elegance to the whole look. Her hair was styled in loose waves that cascaded down her back, and she had applied a light touch of makeup to enhance her natural beauty. Lila felt confident and beautiful as she entered the party with Jess by her side.

Jess was there too, looking stunning in a black dress. She gave Lila a tight hug when she arrived, and they chatted for a while before the party really got going. As the night wore on, the music got louder and people started dancing, and Lila found herself swept up in the excitement of it all.

At one point, Ayla tapped her on the shoulder and handed her a glass of champagne. "Here's to your future, darling," she said, raising her glass. Lila smiled and clinked her glass against Ayla's.

The night was a blur of laughter and conversation, and Lila felt happy and content in the company of her loved ones. As the party started to wind down, she found herself outside on the patio with Jess, looking up at the stars.

"Can you believe it?" Lila said, still in disbelief that she had graduated. "I never thought I'd make it this far."

Jess smiled at her. "You've come a long way, Lila. You should be proud of yourself."

Lila nodded, feeling a sense of accomplishment wash over her. "I am proud. And I'm excited for what's next. I feel like I can do anything now."

Jess took Lila's hand and squeezed it. "You can, Lila. And I'll be here every step of the way." Lila smiled, grateful for Jess's unwavering support. She looked up at the sky, feeling a sense of peace wash over her. The future was uncertain, but for the first time in a long time, Lila felt ready to face it head-on.

Lila had always been ambitious and focused on her studies. Despite the challenges she had faced in her previous college, she was determined to continue her academic journey. She started researching different universities and programs that she could apply for. After much consideration, Lila decided to apply to a prestigious university in another state that was renowned for its academic excellence. She spent weeks working on her application, carefully crafting her essays and gathering all the necessary documents. Finally, the day arrived when she submitted her application. She felt a sense of relief and pride knowing that she had put in her best effort. But the waiting game was just beginning.

Days turned into weeks, and Lila found herself constantly checking her email for updates. She tried to focus on other things, but the anticipation was overwhelming. Then, one afternoon, she received an email from the university. Her heart raced as she clicked on the email, and her eyes scanned the message. She read the first few lines, and a smile broke out on her face. She had been accepted! Lila felt a sense of accomplishment and relief wash over her. She had worked hard and proved to herself that she was capable of achieving her goals. She excitedly called her parents and Jess to share the good news.

When Lila informed her parents about her admission to the new university, they were ecstatic. Ayla and Levin hugged her tightly, congratulating her on her success. They were proud of their daughter and knew that she was destined for great things. Ayla couldn't stop smiling, and Levin was beaming with pride. They both knew how hard Lila had worked to get to this point, and they were thrilled to see her dreams coming true.

"We are so proud of you, Lila. You have worked so hard to get here," Ayla said with tears in her eyes.

Levin patted her on the back and said, "You have made us proud, Lila. We know you will do great things at your new university." Lila was touched by their love and support. She knew that she had made the right decision to pursue further studies, and having her parents' backing made her even more confident.

One day, Lila and Jess were strolling through the college campus, reminiscing about their college days. Lila couldn't believe how much things had changed since she last set foot in the place. She had grown so much, and her life had taken her in such different directions. As they were walking, Lila suddenly heard a familiar voice call out her name. She turned around and saw Mr. Knight standing there, looking as dashing as ever. Her heart skipped a beat at the sight of him.

"Hey, Lila! It's been a while!" Knight said, smiling.

Lila's heart was pounding in her chest as she walked towards him. Jess stood back, giving them space.

"Yeah, it has," Lila replied, trying to keep her voice steady.

"How have you been?" Knight asked, looking at her intently.

"I've been good. Just keeping busy with school and stuff," Lila said, trying to sound nonchalant.

They chatted for a few minutes, catching up on each other's lives. Lila couldn't help but feel a sense of nostalgia as she talked to him. She missed him so much and seeing him again brought back all of the feelings that she had buried deep inside.

As they said their goodbyes and walked away, Lila couldn't help but feel conflicted. She still had feelings for him, but she knew that they could never be together. She had moved on with her life, and she couldn't risk getting hurt again. But as she walked away, Lila couldn't help but wonder what would have happened if things had been different. If they had never been caught, would they still be together? She pushed those thoughts away, knowing that it was pointless to dwell on the past. She had a new life now, and she was excited to see where it would take her.

Fifteen

Dwelling in the past

L ila's new life in the university was vastly different from her old one. She had a newfound confidence, which was reflected in her academic work and her social life. Lila had always been a hard worker, but now she was pushing herself even further. She was taking more difficult classes and participating in extracurricular activities. Lila also made new friends in her new university. She found that she had a lot in common with her classmates and felt a sense of camaraderie with them. They would often study together, go out to eat, or just hang out in the campus quad. Lila felt like she had found her place in the world.

But despite all of the positive changes in her life, Lila still felt a void. She couldn't help but think about Mr. Knight and what could have been. She tried to push those thoughts aside, focusing instead on her studies and her new friends.

One day, Lila was walking to class when she saw a poster for an upcoming writing competition. She had always loved writing and had even written some poetry in her journal, but she had never shared it with anyone. Lila hesitated for a moment, but then decided to take a chance and submit some of her work.

A few weeks later, Lila received an email informing her that she had been selected as one of the finalists in the writing competition. She was thrilled and couldn't believe that her writing had been recognized in such a way.

The night of the competition, Lila was nervous but excited. She had invited her new friends to come and support her. As she walked onto the stage to read her work, Lila felt a rush of adrenaline. She began to read, and as she did, she felt like she was in a trance. The words flowed effortlessly from her lips, and she knew that she had found her calling.

After the competition, Lila's new friends congratulated her and praised her writing. Lila felt like she had finally found her true passion in life. She continued to write and submit her work to various publications, and her writing began to gain recognition.

Despite her growing success as a writer, Lila still couldn't shake off the feeling of missing Mr. Knight. She tried to distract herself with her writing and her new friends, but there was a part of her that still longed for him. One night, as she was writing in her journal, she found herself pouring out all of her thoughts and feelings about him onto the page. She wrote about how much she missed him, how she still loved him despite everything that had happened between them, and how she wished they could find a way to be together again.

As she wrote, tears streamed down her face. She knew that she needed to confront her feelings and figure out what she wanted. She decided to reach out to him and see if they could meet up and talk.

The next day, Lila gathered up all of her courage and called Mr. Knight. Her heart was pounding as she waited for him to answer.

"Hello?" his voice came through the phone.

"Hi, it's Lila," she said, her voice shaking slightly.

There was a pause on the other end of the line before he spoke again.

"Lila, it's so good to hear from you. How have you been?"

"I've been good," she replied. "Listen, I was wondering if we could meet up and talk. There's something I need to say to you."

"Of course," he said. "I'd love to see you."

They arranged to meet up at a coffee shop near Lila's campus the following day. Lila spent the rest of the day trying to calm her nerves and figure out what she wanted to say to him.

When she arrived at the coffee shop, she saw him sitting at a table by the window. He looked up and smiled when he saw her, and Lila felt her heart skip a beat.

They talked for hours, catching up on each other's lives and reminiscing about old times. Lila finally mustered up the courage to tell him how she felt about him.

"I still love you, Mr. Knight," she said. "I don't know if we can ever be together again, but I just wanted you to know how I feel."

He took her hand and looked into her eyes. "Lila, I still love you too. I never stopped loving you."

At that moment, Lila felt like everything was right in the world. They may not have known what the future held, but they both knew that they wanted to be together. Meanwhile, he asked her to give this relationship a chance. She had spent the entire drive back home thinking about him and now he was asking her for another chance. Her mind raced as she tried to process what this meant. She decided to call him back and get some clarity. After a few rings, he answered.

"Hey," he said softly.

"Hey," Lila replied, her heart pounding in her chest.

"I just wanted to talk to you about what happened earlier. I know things didn't end well between us, but I still have feelings for you, Lila. I want to give this another chance, if you'll have me."

Lila felt a mix of emotions. Part of her wanted to jump at the chance to be with him again, but another part of her was scared. She didn't want to get hurt again.

"I don't know, Knight. I need some time to think about this," she finally said.

"I understand. Take all the time you need, Lila. I just wanted you to know how I feel."

They talked a bit more, but Lila was still lost in her thoughts. She was torn between her feelings for him and her fear of getting hurt again.

The next few days were a blur for Lila. She spent most of her time thinking about Knight and what it would mean to give their relationship another chance. She wasn't sure if she was ready to take that risk again.

Finally, after much deliberation, Lila decided to give Knight another chance. She texted him back and agreed to meet him for dinner the following week.

When the day arrived, Lila was nervous but excited. She dressed in her best outfit and made her way to the restaurant. Knight was already there, waiting for her at the table.

As they talked and caught up, Lila realized how much she had missed him. He was still the same person she fell in love with all those years ago, but he seemed different too - more mature and understanding.

After dinner, Knight walked Lila to her car. He took her hand and looked deep into her eyes.

"I know I messed up before, Lila. I'm not perfect, but I promise to be there for you and make this work. Will you give me another chance?" he asked.

Lila felt a lump form in her throat as she looked at him. She knew deep down that she still loved him and wanted to be with him.

"Yes, Knight. I'll give us another chance," she finally said, feeling a weight lifted off her shoulders. Knight smiled and leaned in to kiss her. As they kissed, Lila felt like everything was falling back into place. She had found love again, and this time, she was determined to make it work.

Sixteen

Convoluted plot

Weekend came and Lila went to her home. As Lila settled into her old room, she couldn't help but feel conflicted. On one hand, she was thrilled to be back with Knight, but on the other hand, she knew that her parents had different plans for her.

As she sat at the dinner table with her parents and Knight, her mother spoke up. "Lila, we have been thinking that it's time for you to get married. You're not getting any younger, and we want you to settle down."

Lila felt a knot form in her stomach. She knew this conversation was coming, but she had hoped that her parents would understand that she wanted to focus on her career first. "Mom, I appreciate your concern, but I'm not ready for marriage yet. I want to focus on my writing and my studies," she said, hoping to persuade her parents.

Her father spoke up next. "Lila, we understand that you have dreams, but you need to understand that we only want what's best for you. And in our culture, getting married at your age is the norm. Besides, Knight seems like a good match for you."

Lila looked over at Knight, who was silently eating his food. She knew that her parents meant well, but the idea of getting married to someone she barely knew was not what she had in mind.

"Please, let me focus on my studies for now. I promise I'll consider it in the future," Lila pleaded.

Her parents exchanged a look and then nodded. "Fine, but don't take too long. We want to see you settled down," her mother said, and Lila couldn't help but feel a pang of guilt.

As dinner came to an end, Lila excused herself to her room. She knew that her parents meant well, but she couldn't shake off the feeling that they were pressuring her into something she wasn't ready for. She also couldn't help but wonder what Knight's thoughts were on the matter. Would he be okay with getting married so soon? Or was he just going along with what her parents wanted?

Lost in her thoughts, Lila jumped as her phone buzzed. It was Knight, and her heart skipped a beat. She opened the message and read it carefully.

"I know this might be sudden, but I want to make things official between us. Will you be my girlfriend?"

Lila felt a wave of happiness wash over her. She couldn't believe that Knight felt the same way she did. She quickly typed out her response, "Yes, I will."

As she drifted off to sleep that night, Lila couldn't help but feel excited about the future with Knight. But at the same time, she couldn't ignore the fact that her parents' expectations still weighed heavily on her mind. She knew that she had to find a way to balance her dreams with her family's wishes.

Lila and Mr. Knight had been planning a weekend getaway for a while. They both decided to go on a trip to the mountains, which Lila had always wanted to visit. However, Lila knew that her parents would never approve of her going on a trip with Mr. Knight, so she had to lie to them.

She told her parents that she was going on a trip with her friends and would be back by Monday. Her parents were hesitant at first, but Lila convinced them that she would be safe and would keep in touch throughout the trip.

As they drove up the winding roads to the mountain cabin, Lila felt a rush of excitement and nervousness. She had never been on a trip like this with Mr. Knight before, and she wasn't sure what to expect.

When they arrived, they were greeted by the stunning view of the snow-capped mountains and the cozy cabin they would be staying in. Lila couldn't believe how beautiful it was.

They spent the day exploring the area and taking in the breathtaking scenery. They hiked through the forest, sat by a river, and had a picnic with the view of the mountains. Lila felt more alive than ever before, and she was grateful to be sharing this experience with Mr. Knight.

As the sun began to set, they returned to the cabin and sat by the fireplace. Lila snuggled up next to Mr. Knight, feeling a warmth in her heart that she had never felt before.

They spent the rest of the weekend exploring the mountains and each other. Lila knew that their relationship was risky, but being with Mr. Knight felt right. She was willing to take the chance and see where their love would take them.

Seventeen

Flaming soul

Lila and Mr. Knight's relationship continued to grow more serious as they spent more time together. They went on dates, took trips, and explored new things together. They were always mindful of the risks involved, but they both knew that they couldn't ignore the strong feelings they had for each other. As the months went by, Lila and Mr. Knight became inseparable. They spent every moment they could together, talking about their hopes and dreams for the future. Lila had never felt so understood and loved before, and she knew that Mr. Knight felt the same way.

But even though they were happy, there was always a shadow hanging over their relationship. Lila's parents still didn't approve of their relationship and would often try to persuade Lila to break it off. Lila would try her best to ignore their comments, but deep down, she knew that it was only a matter of time before they would have to confront the issue head-on.

Despite the challenges they faced, Lila and Mr. Knight continued to cherish their time together. They found solace in each other's arms, and for a while, nothing else seemed to matter. They were happy and in love, and that was all that mattered to them.

Lila had just come home from her trip with Mr. Knight when her mother approached her with a stern look on her face. "Lila, I need to talk to you," her mother said, her voice tinged with anger. Lila's heart sank as she followed her mother into the living room. She had a feeling she knew what was coming. She had tried to keep her relationship with Mr. Knight a secret from her parents, but now it seemed like her cover was blown. Her mother sat down on the couch and held up Lila's phone. "Do you want to explain to me what this is?" she asked, gesturing to a picture of Lila and Mr. Knight standing on a mountaintop, arms wrapped around each other. Lila felt her face turn red with embarrassment. "I can explain," she began, but her mother cut her off.

"You lied to us, Lila," her mother said, her voice shaking with anger. "You told us you were going on a trip with your friends, but you were really with this man."

"He's not just any man," Lila protested. "He's Mr. Knight, and we're in love."

"In love?" her mother repeated, incredulously. "Lila, this man is twice your age. He could go to jail for what he's doing."

"It's not like that," Lila said, her voice trembling. "We're just two people who care about each other." Her mother shook her head. "I don't want to hear it, Lila. This is not what we raised you to do. You need to break things off with this man and focus on your studies." "But I love him," Lila said, tears streaming down her face. "I can't just turn off my feelings like that."

"Lila, please," her mother pleaded. "We just want what's best for you. You can't continue down this path. It's not healthy, and it's not safe." Lila knew her mother was right, but it didn't make the situation any easier. She loved Mr. Knight with all her heart, and the thought of breaking things off with him was unbearable. But she also knew that she couldn't keep lying to her parents and risking Mr. Knight's freedom. As she left the room, Lila knew that she had some tough decisions to make.

Lila sat in her room, staring blankly at the wall. Her mother's words kept echoing in her mind. She had never seen her mother so angry before. She felt like she had disappointed her parents by being in a relationship with Mr. Knight. Just then, her phone rang, and she saw that it was Knight calling. She took a deep breath and answered the call. "Hey," she said softly.

"Lila, are you okay?" Knight asked, concern evident in his voice.

Lila sighed. "No, not really. My parents found out about us, and they're furious. They're threatening to report you to the authorities."

Knight was quiet for a moment before he spoke. "I'm sorry, Lila. I never wanted to put you in this position."

"It's not your fault," Lila replied. "I just don't know what to do. They won't listen to me. They think you're some kind of criminal."

Knight's voice was filled with emotion as he spoke. "Lila, I love you. And I promise I will do everything in my power to make things right. I won't let anything come between us."

Lila felt a warmth spreading through her as she heard Knight's words. "Thank you," she whispered. "I love you too." They talked for a while longer, Knight offering words of comfort and support. When they finally hung up, Lila felt like she could breathe a little easier. She knew that things were still uncertain, but she also knew that Knight was there for her no matter what.

Eighteen

Vigorous decision

Lila had been avoiding Jess's calls and messages for a few days, and Jess was starting to get worried. She decided to drive down to Lila's hometown to check on her friend in person. As she knocked on Lila's door, she could hear shuffling inside. Finally, after a few moments, Lila opened the door with swollen eyes and a tired expression.

"Lila, what's going on? Why haven't you been answering my calls?" Jess asked as she walked into the living room.

Lila let out a deep sigh and sat down on the couch. She looked up at Jess with a pained expression on her face.

"It's my parents. They found out about me and Knight," Lila said, her voice shaking with emotion.

Jess's eyes widened in surprise and concern. "What did they do?" she asked, sitting down next to Lila.

"They're so angry. They're forbidding me from seeing him, and they even threatened to report him to the authorities," Lila said, tears streaming down her face.

Jess put a comforting arm around Lila and hugged her tightly. "I'm so sorry, Lila. That's terrible. What are you going to do?" Jess asked, her voice full of concern.

"I don't know. I had to take a leave of absence from my new university because of all of this. I feel like everything is falling apart," Lila said, her voice barely above a whisper. Jess hugged her friend even tighter.

"We'll figure it out, Lila. We'll get through this together," Jess said, trying to sound as reassuring as possible. Lila leaned into Jess's embrace and let out a deep sigh.

"Thank you, Jess. I don't know what I'd do without you," Lila said, her voice muffled by Jess's shoulder. Jess hugged her friend tighter and silently promised to do everything she could to help Lila through this difficult time. After Lila shared everything with Jess, Jess could see the stress and sadness on her friend's face. She decided to take Lila out for lunch to help her take her mind off things and maybe even cheer her up.

They went to a cozy little cafe near Jess's apartment. The atmosphere was warm and welcoming, with soft lighting and gentle music playing in the background. Jess ordered their favorite dishes and they chatted about random things, trying to forget the problems in their lives.

But even with the delicious food and pleasant ambiance, Lila couldn't shake off the feeling of being trapped and alone. Jess noticed her friend's mood and decided to bring up the topic that was bothering Lila.

"Lila, I know this is tough for you. But you can't just give up on your dreams and your happiness. You need to stand up for yourself and fight for what you want." Lila looked at Jess with tears in her eyes.

"But Jess, you don't understand. My parents are so strict and traditional. They won't even listen to me. And now they've forbidden me from seeing Knight. I feel like I have no choice but to do what they say." Jess put her hand on Lila's shoulder.

"I do understand, Lila. And I'm here for you. But you have to remember that this is your life, not theirs. You have the right to make your own choices and be with the person you love." Lila nodded, her eyes still watery.

"But how can I do that, Jess? My parents are everything to me. I don't want to disappoint them." Jess took a deep breath.

"I know it's hard. But sometimes, we have to disappoint the people we love to live the life we want. And who knows, maybe they'll come around eventually." Lila smiled weakly.

"Thanks, Jess. I needed to hear that." They finished their lunch, feeling a little better than before. Lila knew she had a lot of thinking to do, but she was grateful for Jess's support and encouragement. She hoped that someday, her parents would understand her choices and accept her happiness. After a lot of hurdles, that night Knight called Lila and they decided something.

Lila and Mr. Knight had been discussing their relationship for a long time, weighing the risks and rewards of going public. They knew that it would be difficult, but they also knew that they couldn't hide their love forever. Finally, they made the decision to go public. They told Lila's parents first, who were upset but ultimately supportive of their daughter's decision. Then, they told Mr. Knight's boss at the school, who was furious.

The news quickly spread throughout the community, and soon everyone was talking about Lila and Mr. Knight. The school board called for Mr. Knight to be fired, citing ethical concerns about a teacher dating a former student. Lila and Mr. Knight were devastated. They had hoped that people would be more understanding and accepting, but instead, they faced backlash and scrutiny from every angle. Despite the backlash, Lila and Mr. Knight continued to see each other. They were determined to stay together, no matter what anyone else thought. They knew that their love was real and that they were meant to be together.

Nineteen

Family greetings

Lila sat down with her parents and took a deep breath. "I want to talk to you about Mr. Knight," she said calmly. Her parents tensed up at the mention of his name, but Lila continued. "I know you're worried about our relationship, but I need you to understand that he's a good person. He's kind, caring, and he treats me with respect. He's been nothing but supportive of me and my dreams."

"But Lila, he's so much older than you. And he was your teacher. We don't think it's appropriate." Her mother spoke up. Lila nodded, understanding their concerns.

"I know it might seem unconventional, but our age difference doesn't matter to us. And as for the teacher-student relationship, we waited until after I graduated and he resigned from his position before we started dating. It's all completely legal and ethical."

Her father still looked skeptical, so Lila pressed on. "Dad, you always taught me to follow my heart and pursue what makes me happy. Mr. Knight makes me happy. Please try to see him the way I do."

There was a moment of silence as her parents considered her words.

Finally, her mother spoke up. "We just want what's best for you, Lila. If you're happy with him, we'll support you." Lila breathed a sigh of relief and smiled.

"Thank you, Mom and Dad. You won't regret it."

Next day, Mr. Knight arrived at Ayla and Levin's house just in time for dinner as her parents invited him. Lila greeted him at the door and led him to the dining room, where her parents were waiting.

"Welcome, Mr. Knight," Ayla said with a smile. "Please have a seat."

Levin poured wine for everyone, and they all began to chat amicably over appetizers. Ayla had made a delicious vegetable tart, which was a hit with everyone. During the main course, the conversation turned to Mr. Knight's work as a teacher, and Lila's parents expressed their admiration for his dedication to his students.

"I remember when Lila was in high school," Ayla said, "she had some really wonderful teachers who inspired her to pursue her passions. I can see that you're one of those teachers, Mr. Knight."

Mr. Knight thanked her for the compliment and added, "I feel very lucky to have students like Lila. She's a talented writer and a thoughtful person."

As they enjoyed the dessert, the conversation turned to Mr. Knight and Lila's relationship. Ayla and Levin both expressed their support for their daughter's decision to be with him, and Mr. Knight thanked them for their understanding.

"I know that our relationship isn't conventional," he said, "but I promise to always treat Lila with the respect and care that she deserves." The evening ended on a warm and positive note, with everyone feeling satisfied and happy.

Twenty

The Backlash

Lila and Mr. Knight knew that going public with their relationship would not be easy, but they never expected the backlash they received. When the school board called for Mr. Knight to be fired, Lila and Knight knew they had to fight back. They hired a lawyer to defend Mr. Knight's job and to fight against the discrimination they faced. They spent countless hours researching and gathering evidence to support their case. During this time, they faced many challenges and obstacles. They received hate mail and threats, and people would stare and whisper when they were out in public. But they refused to give up on each other and on their love.

Despite the difficult times, Lila and Knight stayed strong and supported each other. They knew that their love was worth fighting for and that they were meant to be together. Finally, after months of hard work and dedication, their lawyer was able to present their case and prove that Mr. Knight had not done anything wrong. The school board ultimately dropped their calls for his termination, and Lila and Knight were able to breathe a sigh of relief. Even though they faced discrimination and prejudice, their love had prevailed. They knew that they still had a long road ahead of them, but they were willing to face any challenges that came their way as long as they were together.

Aroma of the wedding

The wedding day had finally arrived, and Lila and Mr. Knight were both filled with excitement and nerves. The ceremony was held in a beautiful outdoor venue surrounded by greenery and blooming flowers. Lila looked stunning in her ivory lace gown, which hugged her figure perfectly and had a delicate train trailing behind her. She wore her hair in loose waves, with a sparkling hairpiece securing a few strands away from her face. Her makeup was natural and radiant, with a subtle pop of color on her lips.

Mr. Knight looked dashing in his black tuxedo, with a crisp white shirt and a black bow tie. His hair was neatly combed back, and his face was freshly shaved. He couldn't take his eyes off Lila as she walked down the aisle, with her father proudly walking her towards him.

The decorations were elegant and understated, with soft shades of pastel flowers arranged in glass vases lining the aisle. The altar was draped in white fabric, with a simple yet stunning floral arrangement at the center. The ceremony itself was filled with emotion, as Lila and Mr. Knight exchanged heartfelt vows and rings, pledging to love and cherish each other for the rest of their lives. They were surrounded by their closest family and friends, who beamed with happiness as they watched the couple exchange their vows.

As Knight stood before the crowd, his eyes fixed on his beautiful bride Lila, his heart swelled with love and gratitude. He cleared his throat and began his speech.

"My dear Lila, from the moment I met you, I knew you were someone special. You have brought so much love, joy, and happiness into my life. And today, as I stand here before you and our loved ones, I want to thank you for being my rock, my confidant, my partner, and my best friend. I feel so blessed to have you in my life and to be able to share this special day with you. I vow to always support you, to love you unconditionally, and to be there for you through the ups and downs of life. As we embark on this new journey together, I promise to always cherish and respect you. I vow to be your partner in all things, and to grow and evolve with you as we build our life together. You are my soulmate, my heart's desire, and my everything. I love you more than words can express, and I cannot wait to spend the rest of my life with you. Thank you for being my wife and for making me the happiest man on earth."

With those heartfelt words, Knight took Lila's hand and the two exchanged their wedding vows, promising to love and cherish each other for all time. Then Lila held the Mike and spoke beautiful words for Knight:

"My dearest Knight, today is the day we have been waiting for, the day we become one. When I first met you, I never would have guessed that I would be standing here, marrying my best friend and soulmate. But here we are, and I couldn't be happier.

You have been my constant support, my rock, through everything. From the day we met in college, to our long-distance relationship, to our fight for our love, you have been unwavering in your love and dedication to me. You have shown me what true love is, and I am so grateful to have you in my life. As we start this new chapter of our lives together, I promise to always stand by your side, to love you unconditionally, to support you through thick and thin, and to cherish every moment we have together. I love you more than words can express, and I can't wait to spend the rest of my life with you."

The crowd erupted into cheers and applause, and the newlyweds shared a sweet kiss, embarking on their happily ever after. After the ceremony, the guests were treated to a delicious reception dinner, complete with a delectable multi-tiered wedding cake. The dance floor was soon filled with guests dancing to lively music, celebrating the joyous occasion.

As the night drew to a close, Lila and Mr. Knight shared a private moment together, reflecting on their journey to this day and the love that brought them together. They knew that they had faced many challenges along the way, but they had come out stronger and more in love than ever before. They were excited to embark on the next chapter of their lives together as husband and wife.

After a long and difficult journey, Lila and Mr. Knight finally tied the knot in a beautiful ceremony surrounded by their friends and family. They had faced discrimination and prejudice, but they never gave up on their love for each other.

Now, they are happily married and enjoying their new life together. Lila continued to pursue her passion for writing and Mr. Knight continued to teach and inspire his students. They supported each other through thick and thin, and their love only grew stronger with time.

Years later, they looked back on their journey and knew that it was all worth it. They were grateful for the struggles they faced because it brought them closer together and made their love even stronger. In the end, Lila and Mr. Knight proved that true love knows no boundaries and that love always conquers all. They lived happily ever after, inspiring others to never give up on their dreams and always follow their hearts.

"Love's Journey"

In life we seek a love that's true,
A bond that weathers trials anew.
With courage and faith we take the leap,
And venture on love's journey deep."

The End

FREE BOOK

Interested in more forbidden love stories, download 10 FREE Short Romance short stories here and sign up for my mailing list to find out when the next book comes out.

https://bit.ly/PawaFreeRomanceBook

OR

Scan the barcode below

THANK YOU

If you enjoyed this book, please share it and it would mean so much to me if you could leave a review here or where you purchased this book.

https://bit.ly/ReviewTheUnlawfulLove

Also, if you have a minute, follow me on Amazon.

https://amzn.to/3ZVPxrI

Thanks again,

Pawa

About the Author

Born in a small town in the midwestern United States, Pawa showed a passion for writing from an early age. She would spend hours crafting stories and poems, often losing track of time as she delved into her imagination.

After completing her undergraduate degree in English literature, Pawa decided to pursue her dream of becoming a writer full-time. She moved to New York City and began working as a freelance writer, taking on any job that came her way to support herself while she worked on her own projects.

Her breakthrough came with the publication of her first novel, which quickly became a bestseller and earned critical acclaim. Since then, she has published several more books, including a collection of short stories and a memoir about her experiences as a writer.

Pawa's writing is known for its vivid imagery and emotional depth. She draws on her own experiences and observations of the world around her to create characters that feel real and relatable. Her work has been praised for its honesty and its ability to touch readers on a deep level.

When she's not writing, Pawa enjoys hiking, traveling, and spending time with her family and friends. She is also actively involved in supporting literary organizations and mentoring aspiring writers.

You can connect with me on:

- https://pawaromance.com
- https://twitter.compawaromance
- https://www.facebook.com/PawaRomance
- https://www.instagram.com/PawaRomance
- https://tiktok.com/@PawaRomance
- https://youtube.com/@PawaRomance
- https://www.pinterest.com/PawaRomance

Subscribe to my newsletter:

- https://bit.ly/PawaFreeRomanceBook

9 798215 816141